First published in Great Britain in 2018 by Pat-a-Cake
This edition published 2019
Copyright © Hodder & Stoughton Limited 2018. All rights reserved
Pat-a-Cake is a registered trade mark of Hodder & Stoughton Limited
ISBN: 978 1 52638 271 9 • 10 9 8 7 6 5 4 3 2 1
Pat-a-Cake, an imprint of Hachette Children's Group,
Part of Hodder & Stoughton Limited
Carmelite House, 50 Victoria Embankment, London EC4Y 0DZ
An Hachette UK Company
www.hachette.co.uk • www.hachettechildrens.co.uk
Printed in China

The Three Little Pigs

Retold by Ronne Randall

Illustrated by Kasia Nowowiejska

Three Little Pigs

Mummy Pig

road

house

door

Big Bad
Wolf

straw

sticks

bricks

Once there were three little pigs who got bigger and bigger.

Those little pigs got so big that they couldn't stay at home.

They needed houses of their own!

So they said goodbye to Mummy Pig and set off down the road.

The first little pig built his house of straw. And as soon as it was finished, the Big Bad Wolf knocked on the door.

"Little pig, little pig, let me in," he said.

"No!" said the little pig. "Not by the hair of my chinny-chin-chin!"

"Then I'll huff and I'll puff and I'll blow your house in!" said the wolf.

And that's just what he did!

The little pig's reedy, weedy straw house just fell to pieces!

Luckily, the little pig escaped and ran to his brother's house. The second little pig had built his house of sticks.

Soon, along came the Big Bad Wolf.

"Little pigs, little pigs, let me come in," he shouted.

"No!" said the little pigs. "Not by the hairs of our chinny-chin-chins!"

"Then I'll huff and I'll puff and I'll blow your house in!"
roared the wolf.

And that's just what he did! He huffed and he puffed, and he puffed and he huffed . . . and that rickety, clickety house of sticks just tumbled to the ground!

Luckily, the clever pigs had run out of the back door. They ran all the way down the road to their sister's house. She had built her house of bricks.

"Come in quickly!" she said.
"Sit by the fire and get warm!"

Before long, the Big Bad Wolf came along. "Little pigs, little pigs, let me come in!" he bellowed.

"No!" cried the little pigs. "Not by the hairs of our chinny-chin-chins!"

"Then I'll huff and I'll puff and I'll blow your house in!" thundered the wolf.
So he huffed and he puffed . . . and he puffed and he huffed . . .

But no matter how he huffed and how he puffed, he could not budge that strong and sturdy house of bricks!

"I'll get those pigs!" said the wolf. "I'll climb down the chimney!"

The wolf zipped down the chimney . . . and landed bottom-first in the fire!

"Ow! Ow! Ow!" he cried. He ran out of the door and down to the river to bathe his burnt bottom. He never, ever came back.

The three little pigs lived happily ever after,
safe and sound in their sturdy house of bricks.

Storytime Scramble

Here are some pictures from the story.
Point to them in the order they happened
and try to retell the story.